P9-AQZ-013

WHAT I HEAR

WHAT I HEAR
In My School

By June Behrens

Photographs by Michele and Tom Grimm

A Golden Gate Junior Book
Childrens Press · Chicago

Library of Congress Cataloging in Publication Data

Behrens, June.
  What I hear.

  "A Golden Gate junior book."
  SUMMARY: Illustrates with text and photographs some
of the sounds that you might hear if you stop and listen.
  [1. Sounds—Fiction. 2. School stories] I. Grimm,
Michele. II. Grimm, Tom. III. Title.
PZ7.B388234Wg   [E]   76-9099
ISBN 0-516-08745-2

1 2 3 4 5 6 7 8 9 10 11 12 R 80 79 78 77 76

For Mary Heise, who is a good listener

The photographers wish to thank the boys and girls and the teachers of the following Southern California schools for their generous assistance in making possible the illustrations in this book: El Morro School, Laguna Beach; Palisades School, Capistrano Beach; Wilson School, Santa Ana.

A-tink A-ling. A-tink A-ling.

We stop and look and listen.

When Teacher rings the bell, it is

time to listen.

6

Spat spat. Plop plop plop.

Outside on the play yard we hear sounds.

The jumprope goes spat, spat.

8

The big rubber ball bounces plop, plop, plop.

Pssst. Pssst. Pssst.

Tammy whispers secrets in my ear.

Psst. Whispers tickle.

10

Ping   Ping   Ping

   ding.   ding.   ding.

12

Do you like my song?

I hit high notes and low notes.

When good sounds go together, we hear music.

Muunnnch, crunnch.

Pat and Petunia are in their cage.

Munch, crunch.

14

Can you hear them eating the lettuce?

Squeeeeek..squeeeeek...squeeeeek.

What sound is that?

It's our old play yard gate!

Pling pling. Pling pling.

Sometimes Teacher plays her guitar.

We sing along.

Do you sing with your teacher?

WHOOSH...SH..SH....whoosh.

We have a giant seashell.

Listen. I hear something.

I hear the ocean in the giant shell.

20

Pat pat pat. Pat pat.

We pat the sand to make our tunnel.

A truck will go through and come out here.

22

Tick. Tick. Tick. Tick.

It is our teacher's timer.

It will buzz when work time is over.

24

Buzzzzzzzzzz.

Whoooo..whoooo..whooo.

Carlos has a birthday cake with five candles.

Whooo!

Blow out your candles, Carlos.

Drip drip plink.

That is a happy sound.

The water drops play a little tune.

Scrape, scratch. Scrape, scratch.

Can you hear the chalk as I make letters?

Sh…sh. Sh…sh.

30

That is the sound of the eraser.

Snip. Snip snip. Snip.

We cut with our scissors.

We cut out pictures of good things to eat.

32

CLAP clap. CLAP clap.

Simon says clap your hands.

Clap soft, clap LOUD.

34

Simon says clap four times and stop.

BANG BANG BANG BANG.

I hammer with my right hand.

Dalia hammers with her left hand.

36

BRRRRINNNGGGGGGGG.

The outside bell rings loud and long.

The bell tells everyone it is time

38

to go home.

This unusual book is designed to help very young children develop their listening skills in terms of everyday experience in the school environment. The simple, childlike text will encourage children to identify and then to express in words the sounds they hear most often – the squeak of the play yard gate, the *spat-spat* of the jumprope, the *sh...sh, sh..sh* of the eraser against the blackboard, the *brrring* of the outside bell telling boys and girls it is time to go home. The charming full-color illustrations were specially photographed for the book in a number of multi-racial schools.

JUNE BEHRENS has written many books for very young readers, among them *Can You Walk The Plank?*, *Together*, *How I Feel*, *Who Am I?* and *Colonial Farm*, published by Childrens Press. She is also the author of several titles in the Childrens Press play series, including *Feast Of Thanksgiving* and *The Christmas Magic-Wagon*. A distinguished educator, she has been a reading specialist in one of California's largest public school systems since 1965. A graduate of the University of California at Santa Barbara, with a Master's degree from the University of Southern California, Mrs. Behrens holds a credential in Early Childhood Education and has a rich background of teaching experience at all elementary grade levels. She and her husband make their home in Redondo Beach, California.

MICHELE and TOM GRIMM are talented freelance photographers and writers whose work has appeared in an astonishing variety of magazines and books, ranging from *Play Girl* to the *Christian Science Monitor*, and Grolier's *New Book of Knowledge* to *The Hitch Hiker's Handbook*. They frequently do photographic illustrations for children's books, among them June Behrens' *Can You Walk The Plank?* Their own personal area of interest is travel and to date they have visited more than 110 foreign countries. They live in Laguna Beach, one of Southern California's most picturesque seaside communities.